THE FINAL

Written by Alan Durant
Illustrated by Maggie Roman

Thanks to Inclusive Minds (the CIC supporting and championing inclusion and diversity in children's books) for introducing us to Kay and Gabriella through their network of Inclusion Ambassadors.

Special thanks also to Harrison, Parker and Reegan.

Titles in the Making the Team Series:

The Challenge

The Battle

Up and Running

Paying the Penalty

Taking a Stand

The Final

Badger Publishing Limited
Oldmedow Road,
Hardwick Industrial Estate,
King's Lynn PE30 4JJ

Telephone: **01553 816 082**
www.badgerlearning.co.uk

2 4 6 8 10 9 7 5 3 1

The Final
ISBN 978-1-78837-660-0

Commissioning Editor: Sarah Rudd
Editor: Claire Morgan
Designer: Bigtop Design
Cover: alphaspirit.it/Shutterstock

THE FINAL

Contents

Characters

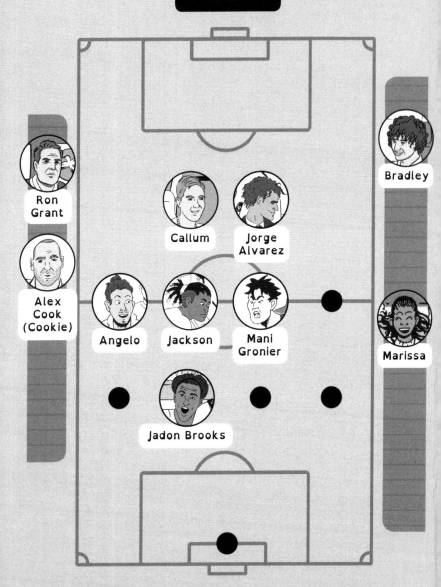

Ron Grant

Alex Cook (Cookie)

Callum

Jorge Alvarez

Angelo

Jackson

Mani Gronier

Jadon Brooks

Bradley

Marissa

Vocabulary

dummied: pretending to pass or shoot to trick the opposition, then doing something completely different to gain an advantage

end-to-end: when both teams are constantly attacking during a match

fourth official: assists the referee and the assistant referee from the side of the pitch

rebounded: when the ball bounces off a goalpost or player

rituals: a series of actions followed in a specific order

snapshot: a type of shot that is taken very quickly by the player, without stopping or controlling the ball

CHAPTER ONE

Seventeen-year-old Callum Cooper opened his eyes in the darkness.

He blinked and frowned for a moment as he tried to work out where he was. Everything was strange.

Then Callum remembered. He wasn't in his bedroom at home or in his shared room by Stanford FC's football ground. He was in a fancy hotel room.

Well, at least it felt fancy to Callum, who had never stayed in his own room in a hotel before.

It was the night before Stanford's final in the Cathay Cup against Roma FC.

Stanford's manager, Ron Grant, had insisted that his First Team squad stay together at a local hotel. He said it would be good for team bonding, but it was more likely that he wanted to make sure no one got into trouble.

Mani Gronier was usually the player who got into trouble, but he wasn't here because he had been suspended for being racist to Callum's friend, Jackson Mbembe.

Callum wasn't going to make a big deal about it, but he was the one who had reported Gronier's behaviour to the manager. He just couldn't stand by and do nothing.

There was no question that Gronier was a great player. He had been vital to Stanford's success, working with Jackson in midfield to turn defence into attack. His passes had helped to create lots of chances for Callum to score, and he would be missed.

But some things were more important than football.

Winger Angelo was great at assisting too, but Callum was worried about him. It seemed like he had an injury and should have some treatment, but the young winger shrugged it off, saying he was fine.

Angelo said he had to play, as half his family were coming over from Italy to watch him.

Callum totally understood why Angelo was so keen to play. All three of them — Callum, Jackson and Angelo — were dying to show off their skills.

A couple of weeks ago, the manager had challenged them to impress him. And they had! Their reward was to play for the First Team.

And now they were in the final of the Cathay Cup!

This final was so exciting — who wouldn't want to play in a cup final against one of Europe's top teams?

But for the three academy players it had an extra edge to it. This was their chance to make their dreams of becoming professional footballers come true.

It had been Callum's dream since he joined Stanford's development team, aged seven.

Many of his friends had given up over the years, but somehow Callum was still here. Now he was on the verge of making it.

Callum got out of bed and opened the curtains. Sunlight beamed in. It was going to be another fine summer's day.

Callum hoped that the sun would shine on him.

CHAPTER TWO

After breakfast, Ron Grant and First Team coach, Alex Cook, nicknamed Cookie, gave a team talk. It was mainly about tactics.

Cookie drew diagrams on a large whiteboard, showing how he wanted the team to play. He wanted the ball to go wide as much as possible.

"We want to see those twinkle-toes of yours, Angelo," Ron Grant said.

Angelo smiled, but he looked tense.

The manager and coach went through set plays, both defending and attacking.

"Make sure you strikers are switched on when Roma have corners and free kicks. We don't want to allow any sloppy goals," barked Cookie.

He was looking straight at Callum when he said this.

Callum blushed. He knew he wasn't great at defending. His skill was in scoring goals, not stopping them.

After being a sub for the first game, he had started the next two and scored against both Porto and AC Milan.

In the last two days, since Stanford had beaten the Italian giants on penalties to reach the Cathay Cup final, Callum's phone hadn't stopped ringing with agents wanting to sign him. He knew it was the same for Jackson and Angelo.

Angelo was keen to sign up at once but Jackson said he needed to talk to his dad first. Jackson's family had to leave their country as refugees because his dad had taken a stand against the government. He had high moral values and thought football agents were just after money.

Callum wasn't against the idea of signing with an agent, but he didn't want to talk to them until after he was offered a pro contract. His dad had once been in the same situation and it had all gone wrong. It had ruined his dad's life and left him bitter and angry. Callum didn't want that to happen to him.

All he wanted at this moment was to beat Roma in the final — and to score the winning goal of course!

For the rest of the morning, the players did their best to relax. Some played games or watched TV, and a few of them went to do some gentle exercise in the hotel gym.

Callum played Xbox with Angelo. It was hard to focus though. He kept imagining how the final would be. The noise of the crowd, the feel of the turf under his boots, the ball at his feet.

Callum's best friend Bradley would be at the front of the crowd with his wheelchair covered in Stanford scarves, banners and badges, cheering him on.

Callum just wanted to be on the pitch now. This waiting was terrible. Was it always like this? Not that he would swap places with anyone else in the world. He knew how lucky he was.

And soon, if all went well, he would be a Premier League footballer. Life surely couldn't get better than that.

CHAPTER THREE

At last, they were on the coach and taking the short drive to the Cathay Arena, Stanford FC's home ground.

The mood was different now, quiet and composed. There was hardly any talk.

Most of the players had their headphones in.

Callum was taking a last look at his phone because checking messages and social media posts was banned in the changing room.

Suddenly, a text popped up that took him totally by surprise. It was from his dad. It said:

Good luck

Callum's heart stopped. He drew a short gasp of breath.

Callum stared at the screen, reading the words over and over again, but not really taking them in. He was in shock.. He hadn't seen or heard from his dad since he had walked out on the family a year ago. As far as he knew, his mum hadn't either.

Callum thought that his dad didn't want to have anything to do with him or his football career. They hadn't parted on good terms so this message was really unexpected. He didn't know what to make of it.

Callum was still deep in his thoughts when the coach arrived at the stadium. He and Angelo were the last to get off. Callum saw his friend wince when he put his left foot down on the ground.

"Are you all right?" he asked, concerned.

"I'm fine," Angelo snapped.

"I can see you've got a problem," Callum persisted. "You have to say something, Angelo."

But Angelo shook his head.

"I can't," he said. "This match is too important. I'll take some painkillers and get treatment when the match is over."

"It's your call," Callum frowned. "But I think you're making a big mistake."

"Just don't say anything, Callum," Angelo begged.

"Fine," Callum sighed. He hoped that Angelo would make it through the game okay.

The heaviness in Callum's heart lifted when he walked into the changing room and saw his shirt hanging there on its peg, waiting for him:

COOPER 19

He would never get tired of seeing that.

Callum picked up the shirt and turned it around so that he could see the club's badge — a bird inside a circle, wings outstretched.

Callum kissed the badge, as he had each time he'd worn the Stanford shirt so far.

Bradley, the club's number one fan, had told him all about the 'good luck' rituals of the Stanford players. Now, Callum had added one of his own.

Ron Grant's pre-match team talk was simple. He told his players to go out and win.

"Do it for the club, do it for the fans, do it for yourselves," he urged. "But most of all, do it for me, because I can't stand that smug, arrogant manager of theirs."

His words brought laughter and broke the tension in the changing room.

Stanford's captain, Jadon Brooks, drew his teammates into a huddle.

"This is it, lads," he muttered. "Let's get out there and show those Roma guys the Stanford spirit."

The team chanted, "Stanford! Stanford!"

They followed Jadon Brooks to the tunnel.

As he followed his teammates out into the sunlight, Callum was met with the loudest roar he had ever heard.

CHAPTER FOUR

Pre-season games didn't usually draw big crowds, but today the Cathay Arena was full.

Several thousand Roma fans had made the trip from Italy and were waving their red and yellow flags and scarves. The rest of the stadium was a swirling sea of Stanford blue and white. The air was filled with noise and excitement.

Lining up for the kick-off, Callum's spine tingled. For years, he'd seen big games like this on TV and wondered what it would be like to play in one. Now, he was finally going to find out.

The ref blew his whistle and the Stanford players took the knee to show they were against racism. Then the ref blew again.

It was kick-off time!

Both teams made a fast start and, for ten minutes, the play was end-to-end. There were a couple of long-range shots, but no clear chances. Neither team was able to take control and the ball was won and lost many times.

Then the game started to calm down. It became careful with lots of passes going sideways and backwards. No one wanted to make a mistake.

The ball was mainly in midfield where Jackson worked hard as always, chasing, making tackles and breaking up the Roma play. But it was proving difficult to get passes through to Callum and his fellow attackers.

On the wing, Angelo grew more and more frustrated. Roma's right full back was a Brazilian international, well-known for his attacking skills. He kept Angelo on his toes, who spent most of the first half running back towards his own goal rather than attacking the Roma goal. Callum felt sorry for him, especially as he was carrying an injury.

There wasn't much in it, but Roma had the edge. Their striker hit the top bar with a snapshot and Brooks booted it up the other end, away from Stanford's keeper. The closest Stanford came to scoring was a header by striker Reegan Keller, but the Roma goalie tipped it over the bar.

Callum couldn't get into the game at all. The few times the ball did come his way, his marker, Roma's captain, beat him to it. He was a classic Italian defender, huge and strong and knew all the tricks in the book. Callum couldn't get past him. He hardly touched the ball in the first half.

When the teams went off at half-time, he was worried that the manager would sub him off.

Ron Grant was never happy at half-time, even when his team was ahead. He often swore and shouted and kicked things across the changing room. He wasn't happy today, but he wasn't angry either. Still, he demanded more from his team — Angelo and Callum in particular.

"Lads, you're letting this team bully you," he said. "I want to see more strength and fighting spirit."

Callum knew he was lucky to still be on the pitch. He would have to do more.

CHAPTER FIVE

The manager's words may have had a positive effect on Callum, but not on Angelo. He was grumbling as they jogged out together for the second half.

"I've been running around after that ball the whole game," he moaned. "What more does he want from me?"

"I guess he wants us to get forward more," Callum suggested.

"That's easy for him to say." Angelo said, as he threw his hands in the air.

Callum had never seen Angelo like this. He suspected it was because he was in pain. He shouldn't have been on the pitch at all.

Angelo's anger started to show in his play. Twice in just a few minutes, he fouled the Roma full back, the second time with a wild lunge that got him a yellow card.

Jackson ran over to him. "Take it easy, Angelo," he said. "Just run with him. Leave the tackling to me."

He put his hand on Angelo's shoulder, but Angelo just shrugged it off. Jackson turned to Callum with a worried frown.

Midway through the second half, Stanford had a huge slice of luck. They took the lead with a shot from Reegan Keller that was going wide until it bounced off a defender's back, sending it into the opposite side of the Roma goal. The keeper didn't have a chance.

Keller looked embarrassed, but his teammates didn't care. They jumped on him in happy celebration, Callum among them.

1–0 to Stanford.

The lead didn't last long, though. Only minutes later, an attack down Roma's right side opened up Stanford's defence. The Brazilian full back dashed forwards into a space, leaving Angelo standing. His powerful shot zoomed into the net. Roma had equalised! The Roma fans jumped and cheered in delight. Angelo hung his head.

As the Stanford players plodded into position for the kick-off, the fourth official was already out on the touchline with his board up. Angelo was off. There was no point in pretending now. Angelo limped to the touchline, shaking his head.

Roma sensed victory now. They attacked with a new energy, but Stanford stood firm. Jadon Brooks was like an iron giant in the heart of the defence and Jackson was everywhere. Callum was amazed by his stamina. It was motivation for the rest of the team.

Suddenly, Callum's legs felt less heavy. He took up wider positions, pulling the Roma captain away from the centre, which left more space for his fellow strikers, Keller and Jorge Alvarez, who'd come on for Angelo. Alvarez nearly took advantage but his forceful shot crashed against the bar.

There were only moments left now and it looked as though the match was going to penalties, as there was to be no extra time.

Once again, for about the thousandth time, Jackson made a great tackle. He won the ball. The play was really spread out now and Jackson found himself with a wide patch of empty turf before him. No one but Jackson would have had the energy to make use of it, but he was off, sprinting forwards. The Roma defence backed off. Jackson was almost up to their penalty box now.

In that split second, Callum knew what was going to happen. It was an exact repeat of a move from the final training practice match before the tournament.

Alvarez made a sudden dart across the goal and the Roma captain moved to cover him. Jackson dummied to make the pass, but then slipped the ball the other way to Callum. Callum reacted quickly.

He reached the ball before anyone else, and, as the keeper came to meet him, slid the ball towards the corner of the goal. He half raised his arm in celebration, then gasped as the ball hit the post, then fell to his knees as it rebounded over the line and into the Roma net! Callum was knocked to the ground as his teammates fell on him in celebration.

Seconds later, the final whistle blew. Stanford had won the Cathay Cup! Callum had scored the winning goal!

Callum and Jackson hugged each other. Then Callum ran over to Bradley and hugged him too.

"You did it!" Bradley shouted with joy.

"We did," Callum yelled in triumph.

Taking off his shirt and handing it to his best friend, Callum grinned, "Here's another one for your collection!"

Bradley smiled. "You'll have to sign it, you know, Callum."

"All in good time," Callum said. "First, I've got a winner's medal to collect."

CHAPTER SIX

"Well, lads, we have done well, haven't we?" Ron Grant smiled.

Callum liked the manager but he didn't trust that smile. Sometimes it felt friendly, but other times it came across as sarcastic.

Callum, Jackson and Angelo were back in Grant's office. The first time they had been here, just a few weeks ago, the manager had given them a challenge.

The second time they'd been here, they'd been told they'd passed the challenge.

Now they were here for a third time, the day after they had played for the Stanford team and won the Cathay Cup.

Callum had high hopes that they were here for something good.

"I'm delighted with the role you young men played in the tournament," the manager said, "and I know Cookie agrees."

First Team coach, Alex Cook, nodded.

"And, as you will know," Grant continued, "he is not an easy man to impress."

Callum agreed. He remembered a lot of shouting during training.

"We think that all three of you could make very fine players," Grant said. He paused and his eyes grew harder. "However, I don't want you to think you're there yet. You still have plenty to learn."

That was probably aimed at me, Callum thought.

"Anyway, Cookie and I have decided to award Jackson a professional contract."

Jackson beamed.

"Well done, lad," said Cookie.

"Angelo..."

Callum's heart felt like a stopped clock. Angelo hadn't made it. He was going to be let go.

"Angelo, you are one of the most naturally talented footballers we've seen," said Grant. "But you need to do a bit of growing up. Not telling us you were injured before the match could have cost the team the entire match."

The manager continued, "So, we want you to go away, get fit and play some more games for the Under-21s. Then we will meet again. Okay?"

Fighting back tears, Angelo nodded. He knew he had made a mistake. He had apologised to Callum lots of times after the match.

Angelo managed a smile at Callum and Jackson before slipping out of the door.

Grant turned his attention to Callum. He wasn't smiling.

"Son," he began, "you need to work on your fitness *and* your strength *and* your control. Your movement could be better too."

The stopped clock in Callum's heart still wasn't ticking.

"But you can score goals. Boy, can you score goals. You're like a young Alvarez. And that's the biggest compliment I could pay you," Grant said.

Now, he did smile. "You've earned yourself a pro contract, young man."

He shook Callum's hand and Cookie did the same. Now it was like Callum's heart was full of clocks ticking and ringing and buzzing.

He'd made it! He'd made the team!

This was it, what he'd strived for all these years at the academy. He was a professional Premier League footballer.

His dream had come true!

Further activities

1 The final match between Stanford and Roma is gripping and fast paced. Write a match report that details the events of the match as they happen.

2 Choose a character from Callum, Jackson or Angelo and write a short story about what happens next in their football career.

Enjoyed this book?

Follow the Making the Team journey
across all six brilliant stories!